Frank Gilbert

Jethro Wood, Inventor of the Modern Plow

A brief account of his life, services and trials - together with facts

subsequent to his death, and incident to his great invention

Frank Gilbert

Jethro Wood, Inventor of the Modern Plow
A brief account of his life, services and trials - together with facts subsequent to his death, and incident to his great invention

ISBN/EAN: 9783337094645

Printed in Europe, USA, Canada, Australia, Japan

Cover: Foto ©Raphael Reischuk / pixelio.de

More available books at **www.hansebooks.com**

JETHRO WOOD,

INVENTOR OF THE

MODERN PLOW.

A BRIEF ACCOUNT OF HIS LIFE, SERVICES, AND TRIALS;

TOGETHER WITH FACTS SUBSEQUENT TO

HIS DEATH, AND INCIDENT TO

HIS GREAT INVENTION.

"No citizen of the United States has conferred greater economical benefits on his country than Jethro Wood—none of her benefactors have been more inadequately rewarded."—*Wm. H Seward.*

By FRANK GILBERT.

CHICAGO:
RHODES & McCLURE.

1882.

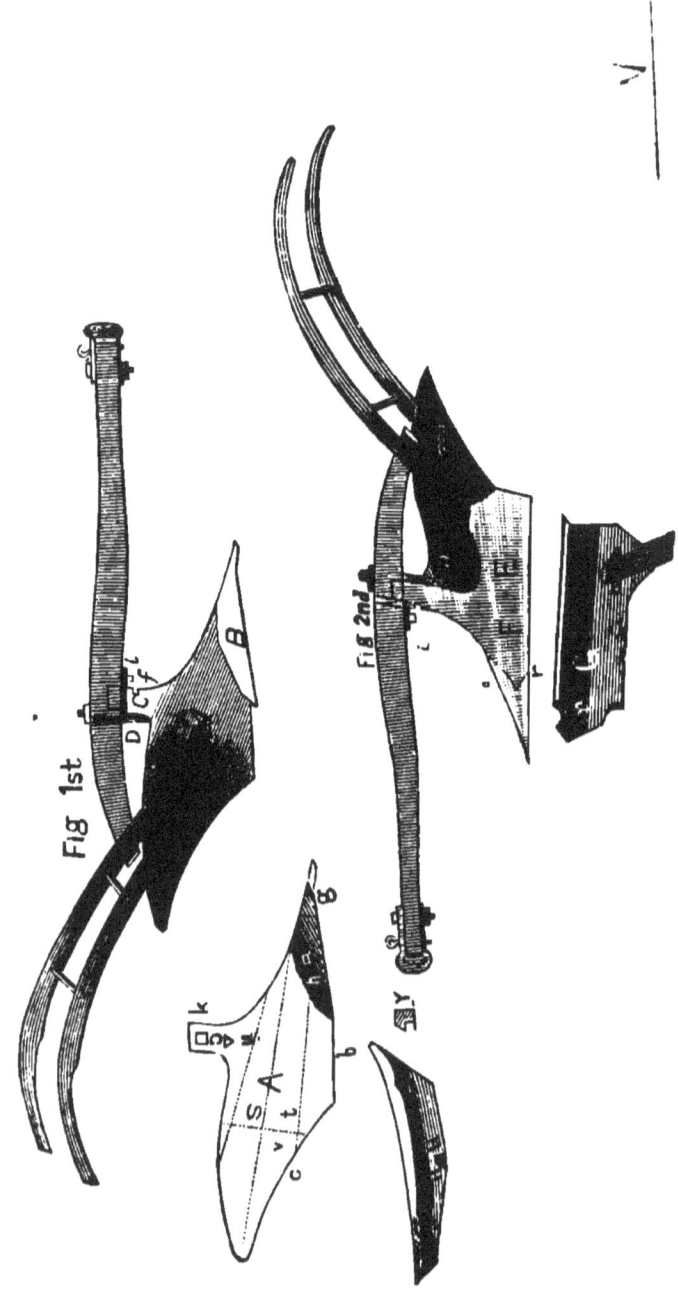

Fig 1st

Fig 2nd

FAC-SIMILE OF THE ORIGINAL WOOD PLOW.

EXPLANATION OF THE FOREGOING FAC-SIMILE.

SIDE VIEW of Plough. *A* M uld-board, the form of which is claimed as new. *B* Share claimed. *C* Standard claimed. *D D* Screw-bolt, and not confining the beam to the Standard. *a, b, c, d, e,* the 1st 2d, 3d, 4th and 5th sides mentioned in the specification. *g, g.* Excavation at the fore part of the mould-board to receive the share which fills it up and forms an even surface. *h* Hole to receive the knob or head cast on the under side of he share, which, on being shoved up to its place, nooks under the mould-board at the upper side of the hole, and is held in its place by a wooden wedge driven between the knob and the lower side of the hole. *f* Notches in the Standard to receive the latch *i* in elevating or depressing the beam. *s, t, v.* Straight diagonal lines touching the mould-board the whole distance. *u* Vertical or plumb line touch ng the mould-board from top to bottom. *H* Reverse side of the share. *x* Knob to hold it fast to the mould-board. *y* Side view of knob. *z z* Shiplaps fitting under the point and edge of the mould-board. *k* Another form of standard keyed on top of beam. Fig. 2d, landside view: *E* The "landside" *F* part of landside cast with mould-board. *m m* Cast loops to hold the handles claimed. *n* Head of screw-bolt held by a shoulder made by a projection from the mould-board and standard, through which the bolt passes up to the beam. *o* Share claimed. *p* Shiplap claimed. *G* Inside view of landside. *r* Tennon at forward end to fit into a dovetailed mortice on the inside of that part which is cast with the mould-board.

(iii)

PREFACE.

THE immediate occasion of this little volume was a malignant misrepresentation from the pen of Ben: Perley Poore. With slight variation from the original text, the words of Thomas Jefferson about Benjamin Franklin and his maligners, quoted in the body of this monograph, apply to this case: I have seen with extreme indignation the blasphemies lately vended against the memory of the father of the American plow. But his memory will be venerated as long as furrows are turned and soil tilled. The present object, however, is not so much to refute falsehood as to establish the truth, and make it a part of the permanent knowledge of the public. To the ex-

(v)

tent that this object shall be attained, will these labors be rewarded.

It is not the design of this publication to disparage any one ; on the contrary, it is desired to give ample credit to all who contributed to the solution of the plow problem. If only brief mention is made of others, it is because they really deserved but little credit, or their merits are forever buried in obscurity. It is proposed to set forth without exaggeration, the claims of the supreme inventor in this line to the grateful remembrance of the public. And by the public is meant not only the American people, but all who are fed from the ample granaries of this country, or share the benefits of the improved tillage, whether on this continent or in Europe, made possible and actual by the inventive genius of Jethro Wood.

JETHRO WOOD;
INVENTOR OF THE MODERN PLOW.

THE last words ever penned by John Quincy Adams were these, written in the peculiarly tremulous hand of "the Old Man Eloquent:" "Mr. J. Q. Adams presents his compliments to the Misses Wood, and will be happy to see them at his house, at their convenience, any morning between 10 and 11 o'clock." This note was found upon his desk when he was stricken down with paralysis, February 21, 1848, in his seat in the House of Representatives. The Misses Wood here referred to were the daughters of Jethro Wood, then deceased. They were at that time engaged in a labor of love, and the venerable Ex-President was their friend therein. Prompted more by

(7)

filial affection than by hope of gain, they were making a final effort to secure from Congress a proper recognition of their father's claim as an inventor. It is entirely safe to say that if Mr. Adams had been spared to the end of the Congress then in session, that claim would have been then duly recognized, and the name, services and genius of Jethro Wood become familiar to the American public.

Jethro Wood was born at Dartmouth, Massachusetts, on the sixteenth day of the third month of 1774. His parents were members of the Society of Friends. His mother, Dinah Hussey Wood, was a neice of Ann Starbuck, a woman of remarkable ability and high standing in colonial annals. Ann Starbuck was virtually governor of Nantucket. The neice was a woman of excellent intellect, and most winsome character. Her conversation sparkled with genial wit and good cheer. Her husband, John Wood, was a man of sterling worth, calm, self-poised, strong willed, and eminently influential. Jethro was their only son. On New Years Day, 1793, he was married to Sylvia Howland, at White Creek, Washington County, New York. The fruit of this marriage, every way a happy one, was a family of six children, namely: Benjamin; John; Maria, wife of Jeremiah Foote; Phœbe; Sarah, wife of Robert R. Underhill; Sylvia Ann, wife of Benjamin Gould. Of these children the only survivor is Mrs. Gould, who with her sister, Phœbe, were the Misses Wood of the Adams note. So much for the domestic setting of this diamond of inventive genius.

Even as a boy, Jethro Wood showed plainly the drift and trend of his mind. The child was indeed " father of the man," and almost from the cradle to the grave, he was an inventor. In his childish plays he seemed bus-

ied with the idea which he ultimately per-
fected. Many curious incidents and memories
are treasured among the traditions of his neighbors and friends. "When only a few years
old," writes a venerable man whose recollection spans two generations, "he moulded a little
plow from metal, which he obtained by melting a pewter cup. Then, cutting the buckles
from a set of braces, he made a miniature har-
ness with which he fastened the family cat to
his tiny plow, and endeavored to drive her
about the flower-garden. The good old-fash-
ioned whipping he received for this 'mischief,'
was such as to drive all desire for repeating
the experiment out of his juvenile head."

Such innate and ruling passion might be
suppressed, but could not be subdued. As his
mind matured, his thoughts took definite shape.
His home was always upon a farm, but he was
never a farmer, in the sense of Poor Richard's
homely couplet :

" He who by the plow would thrive,
  Himself must either hold or drive."

Born in comparative affluence, blessed with a good education, an ample library and a well equipped workshop, enjoying the correspondence of such men as Thomas Jefferson and David Thomas, he was unremitting in his endeavor to realize his ideal. " His chief desire," to quote further from our venerable correspondent, " was to invent a new mold-board, which, from its form, should meet the least resistance from the soil, and which could be made with share and standard, entirely of cast iron. To hit upon the exact shape for the mold-board he whittled away, day after day, until his neighbors, who thought him mad on the subject, gave him the soubriquet of the " whittling Yankee." His custom was to take a large oblong potato which was easy for the knife, and cut it till he obtained what he fancied was the exact curve."

The manhood home of Jethro Wood was at Scipio, Cayuga County, New York, a purely agricultural town, with nothing in its later history to distinguish it; but in its palmier early days of the present century, it must have been a nursery of invention. Roswell Toulsby, Horace Pease, and John Swan, of that town, each took out letters patent for improvements in plows, and that prior to the issuance of any patent to Mr. Wood. Their improvements were of no practical value, and played no part in the development of this branch of mechanism, but their efforts serve to show the state of the intellectual atmosphere breathed by the man who was destined to solve the knotty problem which underlies the very foundation of scientific agriculture.

Of the cotemporaries of Mr. Wood, who wrought at the solution of this problem, the most illustrious was Thomas Jefferson, statesman, philosopher and farmer.

In one of his letters to Jethro Wood, Mr. Jefferson spoke of his own labors in that direction, as the experiments of one whiling away a few idle hours, but herein he did himself injustice. His efforts, however, were far from exhaustive in their results, and it was with good reason that he urged Mr. Wood to go forward in his undertaking, and no doubt he was perfectly sincere in wishing him success. His correspondence, as published in nine large volumes, attests his long and deep interest in the problem, which it was reserved for Jethro Wood to solve. Having carefully examined those volumes, to glean all there is in them on this subject, I herewith append the observations found, for besides being in themselves interesting, in view of their authorship, they throw important light upon the general subject.

Under date of July 3, 1796, Mr. Jefferson wrote to Jonathan Williams: "You wish me

2

to present to the Philosophical Society the result of my philosophical researches since my retirement. But, my good Sir, I have made researches into nothing but what is connected with agriculture. In this way I have a little matter to communicate, and will do it ere long. It is the form of a mould-board of *least resistance.* I had some years ago conceived the principle of it, and I explained it then to Mr. Rittenhouse. I have since reduced the thing to practice, and have reason to believe the theory fully confirmed. I only wish for one of those instruments used in England for measuring force exerted in the drafts of different ploughs, etc., that I might compare the resistance of my mould-board with that of others. But these instruments are not to be had here. In a letter of this date to Mr. Rittenhouse I mention a discovery in animal history, very signal indeed, of which I shall lay before the society the best account I can, as soon as I shall have received some other materials collecting for me.

" I have seen, with extreme indignation, the blasphemies lately vended against the memory of the father of American philosophy. But his memory will be venerated as long as the thunder of heaven shall be heard or feared."

March 27, 1798, Jefferson wrote to Mr. Patterson: " In the life time of Mr. Rittenhouse, I communicated to him the description of a mould-board of a plough, which I had constructed, and supposed to be what we might term the *mould-board of least resistance.* I asked not only his opinion, but that he would submit it to you also. After he had considered it he gave me his own opinion that it was demonstratively what I had supposed, and I think he said he had communicated it to you. Of that however, I am not sure, and therefore, now take the liberty of sending you a description

of it, and a model which I have prepared for
the Board of Agriculture of England, at
their request. Mr. Strickland, one of their
members, had seen the model, also the thing
itself in use on my farm, and thinking favorably
of it, had mentioned it to them. My purpose
in troubling you with it is to ask you to ex-
amine the description rigorously, and suggest
to me any corrections or alterations which you
may think necessary. I would wish to have
the idea go as correctly as possible out of my
hands. I had sometimes thought of giving it
into the Philosophical Society, but I doubted
whether it was worthy of their notice, and supposed it not exactly in the line of their publi-
cations. I had therefore contemplated sending
it to some of our agricultural societies, in
whose way it was more particularly, when I received the request of the English board. The
papers I enclose you are the latter part of a
letter to Sir John Sinclair, their president. It

is to go off by packett, wherefore I wish to ask
the favor of you to return them with the model
in the course of the present week, with any
observations you will be so good as to favor
me with."

Writing from Washington, July 15, 1808,
to Mr. Sylvestre, in acknowledgment of a
plow received from the Agricultural Society
of the Seine (France), he adds: "I shall
with great pleasure attend to the construction
and transmission to the society of a plough with
my mould-board. This is the only part of
that useful instrument to which I have paid
any particular attention. But knowing how
much the perfection of the plough must depend,
1st, on the line of traction; 2d, on the direction of the share; 3d, on the angle of the
wing; 4th, on the form of the mould-board;
and persuaded that I shall find the three first
advantages eminently exemplified in that
which the society sends me, I am anxious to

see combined with these a mould-board of my
form, in the hope it will still advance the perfection of that machine. But for this I must
ask time till I am relieved from the cares
which have more right to all my time—that
is to say, till next spring;" *i. e.* until after
the expiration of his second term as President
of the United States.

The importance of any step in civilization
can be understood only in its relations, ante-
cedent causes and actual results.

The *Scientific American,* which is certainly
good authority in such matters, ranks Jethro
Wood with Benjamin Franklin, Eli Whitney,
Robert Fulton, Charles Goodyear, Samuel B.
Morse, Elias Howe, and Cyrus H. McCormick,
and these are certainly the great names and this
a just classification. Each in his way laid the
foundation on which all inventors in his re-
spective line have built, and must continue to
build, and none of them all came so near per-

fecting his grand idea as Mr. Wood. His now venerable daughter stated the exact truth when she remarked in a letter not designed for publication: "My father patented the shape and construction of the plow. He took the iron and shaped the plow that turns the furrow for every product of the soil in America. His plow has never been improved. It came from his hand simple and perfect, as it now is, and there is no other plow now in use." It was not the use of cast iron that he invented, although the use of "pot metal" by him occasioned a great deal of hostility to the original Wood plow.

Jethro Wood took out two plow patents, and those who wish to belittle his work, descant upon the first as if it were his only claim to credit. That first patent was issued in 1814. It fell far short of satisfying the patentee's ambition. The plows made under it must have been a great improvement on any then in use, for although he abandoned it almost from the first, a great many of them were sold during the period between the first and the second patents. The second patent dates from 1819. The natal day of the modern plow may be fairly set down as September 1, 1819. The original specifications in this plow deserve to be given in full, and may well be inserted in this connection. The document was the handiwork of Mr. Wood himself, and runs thus :

" The Schedule referred to in these Letters Patent, and making part of the same, containing a description in the words of the said Jethro Wood himself of his improvement in the construction of Ploughs.

" Considering the manifold errors and defects in the construction of Ploughs, and the inconveniences experienced in the use of them, the petitioner and inventor hath applied the powers of his mind to the improvement of this noble utensil, and produced a Plough so far superior to those in common use, that he asks an exclusive privilege for the same from the government of his country.

" The principal matters for which he solicits Letters Patent, he now reduces to writing, and explains in words and sentences as appropriate and significant as he possibly can. But, being perfectly aware of the feebleness and insufficiency of language to convey precise and adequate ideas of complicated forms and proportions, the said Jethro Wood annexes to these presents, a delineation upon paper of his said new and improved Plough, with full and explanatory notes; urging with earnestness and respect that the delineation and notes may be considered as a part of this communication. The said petitioner and inventor also, being perfectly convinced, as a practical man, that a model of his inventions and improvements will convey and preserve the most exact and durable impressions of the matters to which he lays claim, he sends herewith a model of the due form and proportion of each, as a just exhibition of his principle and of its application to the construction and improvement of the Plough, requesting that the same may be kept in the Patent Office, as a perpetual memorial of the invention and its use.

In the first place, the said Jethro Wood claims an exclusive privilege for constructing the part of the Plough, heretofore, and to this day, generally called the mould-board, *in the manner hereinafter mentioned.* This mould-board may be termed a plano-curvilinear figure, not defined nor described in any of the elementary books of geometry or mathematics. But an idea may be conceived of it thus:

"The land-side of the Plough, measuring from the point of the mould-board, is two feet and two inches long. It is a strait-lined surface, from four to five and one-half inches wide, and half an inch thick. Its more particular description will be hereinafterwards given. It is sufficient to observe here, that of the twenty-six inches of length on the land-side, eighteen inches belong to the part of the Plough strictly called the land-side, and eight inches to the mould-board. The part of the mould-board comprehended by this space of eight inches is very important, affording weight and strength and substance to the Plough; enabling it the better to sustain the cutting-edge for separating and elevating the soil or sward, and likewise the standard for connecting the mould-board with the beam, as will hereinafter be described more at large.

"The figure of the mould-board, as observed from the furrow-side, is a sort of irregular pentagon, or five-sided plane, though curved and inclined in a peculiar manner. Its two lower sides touch the ground, or are intended

to do so, while the three other sides enter into
the composition of the oblique, or slanting
mould-board, over-hanging behind, vertical
midway, and projecting forward. The angle
of the mould-board, as it departs from the
foremost point of, or at, the land-side, is about
forty-two degrees, and the length of it, or, in
other words, of the first side, is eleven inches.
The line of the next, or the second side, is
nearly, but not exactly parallel with the before-
mentioned right-lined land-side, for it widens
or diverges from the angle at which the first
and second sides join towards its posterior or
hindermost point, as much as one inch.
Hence, the distance from the hindermost point
of the mould-board, at the angle of the second
and third sides, directly across to the land-
side, is one inch more than it is from the angle of
the first and second sides, directly across. The
length of this, the second side, is eight inches.
The next side, or what is here denominated

the third side, leaves the ground or furrow in a slanting direction backward, and with an overhanging curve, exceeding the perpendicular outwards from three to six inches, according to the size of the Plough. The length of this third side is fourteen inches and one-half. The fourth side of this mould-board is horizontal, or nearly so, extending from the uppermost point of the third side, to the fore part, or pitch, eighteen inches. The fifth, or last side, descends or slopes from the last mentioned mark, spot, or pitch, to the place of beginning at the low and fore point of the mould-board, where it joins the land side. Its length is thirteen inches.

"Besides these properties and proportions of his mould-board, the said Jethro Wood now explains other properties which it possesses, and by which it may be and is distinguished from every other invented thing. The peculiar curve has been compared to that of the

screw auger; and it has been likened to the
prow of a ship. Neither of these similitudes
conveys the fair and proper notion of the invention.

" The mould-board, which the said Jethro
Wood claims as his own, and which is the
result of profound reflection and of numberless
experiments, is a sort of plano-curvilinear surface, as herein-before stated, having the following bearings and relations: A right line,
drawn by a chalked string or cord, or by a
straight rule, diagonally or obliquely upwards
and backwards from a point two inches and a
half inch above the tip or extremity of the
mould-board to the angle where the third and
fourth sides of the mould-board join, touches
the surface the whole distance, in an even and
uniform application, and leaves no sinking,
depression, hole, cavity, rising, lump, or pro-
tuberance, in any part of the distance. So, at
a distance half way between the diagonal line

just described, and the angle between the first and second sides, a line drawn parallel to the diagonal line already mentioned will receive the chalked string or cord, or the straight rule, as on an uniform and even surface without the smallest bend, sinuosity, or bunch, whereby earth might adhere to the mould-board, and impede the motion and progress of the Plough, under, through and along the soil.

"In like manner, if a point be taken one inch behind the angle connecting the second and third sides, and a perpendicular be raised upon it, that perpendicular will coincide with the vertical portion of the mould-board in that place ; or, in other words, if a plumb line be let fall so as to reach a point one inch behind the last mentioned angle, then such a plumb line will hang parallel with the mould-board the whole way ; the line of the mould-board there, neither projecting nor receding but being both a right line and a perpendicular line.

" Moreover, if a right line be drawn from
a point on the just described perpendicular, an inch, or thereabouts, above the upper
margin of the fourth side, and from the
point to which the said perpendicular, if
continued, would reach ; if, the said Jethro
Wood repeats, a right line be drawn down-
ward and forward, not exactly parallel to the
diagonal herein already described, but so di-
verging from the same that it is one inch more
distant or further apart, at its termination on
the fifth side of the mould-board, than at its
origin or place of beginning ; such line, so
beginning, continued, and ended, is a right
line parallel to the mould-board along its whole
course and direction, and the space over which
it passes has no inequality, hill, or hollow
thereabout.

" Furthermore, an additional property of his
mould-board is, that, if it be measured and
proved various ways, vertically and obliquely,

by the saw in fashioning it, by the rule in meeting it, and by the chalk-line in determining it, the capital and distinguishing character of right lines existing on, over and along the peculiar curve which his mould-board describes, is always and inseparably present. This grand and discriminating feature of his mould-board, he considers as of the utmost importance.

" He therefore craves the aid and elucidation of his drawing, and of his model, in their totality and in their several parts, to render plain and sure whatever there may be, from the abstruse and recondite nature of the subject, uncertain or dubious in the language of his specification.

" In the second place, the said Jethro Wood claims an exclusive right and privilege in the construction of a standard of cast iron, like the rest of the work already described, for connecting the mould-board with the beam.

3

This standard is broad, stout, strong; and
rises from the fore and upper part of the
mould-board, being cast with it, and being a
projection or continuation of the same from
where the fourth and fifth sides meet. Its
figure, strength, and arrangement are such
as best to secure the connexion, and to enable
the standard thus associated with the beam, to
bear the pull, tug, and brunt of service.
By a screw bolt and nut properly adjusted
above the top of the standard and acting
along its side, assisted, if need require,
by a wedge for tightening and loosening,
the beam may be raised and lowered; and the
mould-board, with its cutting edge, enabled to
make a furrow of greater or smaller depth, as
the ploughman may desire, and a latch and
key fixed to the beam, and capable of
being turned into notches, grooves, or depres-
sions on one edge or narrow side of the standard, serves to keep the beam from settling or

descending. By means of these screw bolts, wedges, latches, and keys, with their appropriate notches, teeth, and joggles, the Plough may be deepened or shallowed most exactly.

"In the third place, the said Jethro Wood claims an exclusive privilege in the inventions and improvements made by him in the construction of the cutting edge of the mould-board, or what may be called, in plain language, the plough-share. The cutting edge consists of cast iron, as do the mould-board and land-side themselves. It is about twelve inches and one half of one inch long, four inches and one half of one inch broad, and in the thickest part three quarters of an inch thick. It is so fashioned and cast, that it fits snugly and nicely into a corresponding excavation or depression at the low and fore edge of the mould-board, along the side hereinbefore termed the first side. When properly adapted, the cutting edge seems, by its uni-

formity of surface and evenness of connextion,
to be an elongation of the mould-board, or, as
it were, an extension or continuation of the
same. To give the cutting edge firm coher-
ence and connexion, it is secured to the mould-
board by one or more knobs, pins or heads in
the inner and higher side, which are received
into one or more holes in the fore and lower
part of the mould-board. By this mechanism,
the edge is lapped on and kept fast and true,
without the employment of screws. That the
cutting edge may be the more securely and
immovably kept in its place, it has a groove,
or ship-lap of one inch in length, below, or at
its under side, near the angle between the first
and second sides, for the purpose of holding it,
and for the further accomplishment of the
same object, another groove or ship-lap,
stouter and stronger than the preceding, is
also cast in the iron, at or near the point of
the mould-board, so as to cover, encase, and

protect it effectually, on the upper and lower sides, but not on the land side.

"After the cutting edge is thus adapted and adjusted to the mould-board by means of the indentations, pins, holes, ship-laps, and fastenings, it is fixed to its place and prevented from slipping back, or working off, by wedges or pins of wood, or other material, driven into the holes from the inner and under side, and forced tight home by a hammer.

"In the fourth place, the said Jethro Wood claims the exclusive right of securing the handles of his plough to the mould-board and land-side of the plough by means of notches, ears, loops, or holders, cast with the mould-board and land-side respectively, and serving to receive and contain the handles, without the use of nuts and screws. For this purpose one or more ears or loops, or one or more pairs of notches or holders are cast on the inner side of the mould-board and land side, toward their hinder or back parts, or near their after margins, for the reception of the handles of the Plough. And these, when duly entered and fitted, are wedged in, instead of being fastened by screws.

"In the fifth place, the said Jethro Wood claims an exclusive right to his invention and improvement in the mode of fitting, adapting and adjusting the cast iron landside to the cast iron mourld-board. Their junction is after the manner of tenon and mortice ; the tenon being at the fore end of the land-side and the mortice being at the inside of the mould-board and near its point. The tenon and mortice are joggled, or dove-tailed together in the casting operation, so as to make them hold fast. The fore end of the tendon is additionly secured by a cast projection from the inside of the mould-board for its reception ; and if any other tightening or bracing should be requisite, a wooden wedge, well driven in, will bind every part effectually, and all this is accomplished without the assistance or instrumentality of screws.

" The said inventor and petitioner wishes it to be understood, that the principal metallic material of his Plough is cast iron. He has very little use for wrought iron, and by adapting the former to the extent he has done, and by discontinuing the latter, he is enabled to make the Plough stronger and better, as well as more lasting and cheap.

" He also claims, and hereby asserts the right, of varying the dimensions and proportions of his Plough, and of its several sections and parts, in the relations of somewhat more and somewhat less of length, breadth, thickness, and composition, according to his judgment or fancy, so that all the while he adheres to his principle and departs not from it.

" Regarding each and every of the matters submitted as very conducive to the reputation

and emolument of the said Jethro Wood, he
relies confidently upon a benign and favorable
construction of his petition and specification,
by the constituted authorities of his country.

"Given under his hand, at the city of New
York, this fourteenth day of August, one
thousand eight hundred and nineteen (1819),
in the presence of two witnesses, to wit:

"SAM'L L. MITCHELL, } JETHRO WOOD."
"J. G. BOGERT.   }

This patent expired by its own limitation in
fourteen years, when it was renewed or continued for another term of fourteen years. In
view of the comparative ease and speediness
with which the inventors of the present day,
or their assigns, utilize really valuable patents,
it would be inferred, in the absence of specific
knowledge to the contrary, that twenty-eight
years constituted a sufficiently long period for
the enjoyment by Mr. Wood, of "the full and
exclusive right and liberty of making, con-

structing, using and vending to others to be used," the plow which he had invented. No doubt some members of Congress in refusing to continue the patent for a third term, acted from conscientious motives. But in point of fact, the period was occupied in a series of struggles calamitous to the inventor, to the history of which we must now turn. These struggles were unlike those in the lives of some other great inventors, notably, Goodyear and Howe. It was not a warfare for existence, the wolf of poverty staring him in the face. The broad fields which he had inherited from his father were adequate immunity from the sad fate too frequently allotted to inventors. But no benefactor of mankind in the domain of mechanism ever experienced more iniquitous treatment than Jethro Wood did.

Before the year 1819 closed, his mission as an inventor was an accomplished fact. The popular name given his implement, " The Cast

Iron Plow," from its entire abandonment of
wrought iron in its construction, needed no
change to be the noblest gift ever made to
agriculture. In the ideal, hope had ripened
into full fruition. And now, at this day,
looking at the matter in the light of the past,
seeing the absolutely incalculable benefits
of the invention, it seems almost incredible
that the American people, then even more
than now, a nation of farmers, should not
have hailed the new plow as an unspeakable
boon, especially the community in which he
dwelt, for Cayuga county then, as now,
under a high state of cultivation, was and is
peopled by a population of much more than
average intelligence. But an inventor, like " a
prophet, is not without honor save in his own
country." His neighbors gravely shook their
heads at " Jethro's folly." With almost entire unanimity they agreed that the new con-
trivance would never work. His trials and

difficulties at this stage of progress are told as follows, by one who wrote largely from personal recollection :

" He immediately began to manufacture his plows, and introduce them to the farmers in his neighborhood. The difficulties which he now encountered would have daunted any man without extraordinary perseverance and a firm belief in the inestimable benefit to agriculture sure to result from his invention. He was obliged to manufacture all the patterns, and to have the plow cast under the disadvantages usual with new machinery. The nearest furnace was thirty miles from his home, and, baffled by obstacles which unskillful and disobliging workmen threw in his way, he visited it, day after day, directing the making of his patterns, standing by the furnaces while the metal was melting, and often with his own hands aiding in the casting.

" When, at length, samples of his plow were

ready for use, he met with another difficulty
·in the unwillingness of the farmers to accept
them. 'What,' they cried, in contempt, 'a
plow made of pot metal? You might as well
attempt to turn up the earth with a glass plowshare. It would hardly be more brittle.'

"One day he induced one of the most skep-
tical neighbors to make a public trial of the
plow. A large concourse gathered to see how
it would work. The field selected for the test
was thickly strewn with stones, many of them
firmly imbedded in the soil, and jutting up
from the surface. All predicted that the plow
would break at the outset. To their astonish-
ment and Wood's satisfaction, it went around
the field, running easily and smoothly, and
turning up the most perfect furrow which had
ever been seen. The small stones against
which the farmer maliciously guided it, to test
the 'brittle' metal, moved out of the way as
if they were grains of sand, and it slid around

the immovable rocks as if they were icebergs. "Incensed at the non-fulfillment of his prophecy, the farmer finally drove the plow with all force upon a large bowlder, and found to his amazement that it was uninjured by the collision. It proved a day of triumph for Jethro Wood, and from that time he heard few taunts about the pot-metal.

"It was soon discovered that his plow turned up the soil with so much ease that two horses could do the work for which a yoke of oxen and a span of horses had sometimes been insufficient before; that it made a better furrow, and that it could be bought for seven or eight dollars; no more running to the blacksmith, either, to have it sharpened. It was proved a thorough and valuable success. Thomas Jefferson, from his retirement at Monticello, wrote Wood a letter of congratulation, and although his theory of the construction of mould-boards had differed entirely from the inventor's, gave

his most hearty appreciation to the merits of
the new plow."

In this connection may be told a curious
episode, one in itself worthy of record, and
strikingly illustrative of the perversities of
fortune to Mr. Wood in those gloomy days.
It is the story of a Czar and a Citizen.

All uncertainty as to the feasibility of the
new plow having been removed, and actuated
by that broad philanthropy which was one of
the peculiar charms in the character of Mr.
Wood, he desired to extend as widely as possible the area of his usefulness, and concluded
to make the Czar of Russia, so long the chief
grain exporting country of the world, the
present of one of his plows. During the
Revolutionary war, then fresh in the American
mind, that great sovereign, Catherine of Russia, had been the staunch friend of this country, and that, too, without being impelled by
jealousy of Great Britain. It seems to be a

peculiar trait in the Romanoff family to ad-
mire liberty in the abstract, however absolute
in practice. Sharing the prevailing good
will toward Russia, Mr. Wood conceived this
happy thought of making a truly substantial
contribution to Cossack civilization, a civilization ever ready, with all its crudeness, to adopt
foreign improvements. That gift, in one
point of view slight, proved of great benefit
to Russian agriculture. It is impossible to
state the extent of actual advantage derived by
Russia from that truly imperial gift. It was
in effect giving to that country, second only
to the United States in area of tillage, in proportion to population, the free use of the per-
fected plow. In an old copy of the New
York *Tribune*, in its palmy days of Horace
Greeley and Solon Robinson, the tale of the
Plow and the Ring is unfolded. It runs thus:

"During the year, 1820, Jethro Wood
sent one of his plows to Alexander I,

Emperor of Russia, and the peculiar circum-
stances attending the gift and its reception
formed a large part of the newspaper gossip
of the day. Wood, though a man of cultivation, intellectually as well as agriculturally,
was not familiar with French, which was then
as now the diplomatic language. So he re-
quested his personal friend, Dr. Samuel
Mitchill, President of the New York Society
of Natural History and Sciences, to write a
letter in French to accompany the gift.

"The autocrat of all the Russias received
the plow and the letter, and sent back a diamond ring—which the newspapers declared
to be worth from $7,000 to $15,000—in token
of his appreciation. By some indirection, the
ring was not delivered to the donor of the
plow, but to the writer of the letter, and Dr.
Mitchill instantly appropriated it to his own
use. Wood appealed to the Russian Minister
at Washington for redress. The Minister

sent to his Emperor and asked to whom the ring belonged, and Alexander replied that it was intended for the inventor of the plow. Armed with this authority, Wood again demanded the ring of Mitchill. But there were no steamships or telegraphs in those days, and Mitchill declared that in the long interval in which they had been waiting to hear from Russia, he had given it to the cause of the Greeks, who were then rising to throw off the yoke of their Turkish oppressors. A newspaper of the time calls Mitchill's course "an ingenious mode of quartering on the enemy," and the inventor's friends seem to have believed that the ring had been privately sold for his benefit. At all events it never came to light again, and Wood, a peaceful man, a Quaker by profession, did not push the matter further."

Perhaps another and quite as potent a reason why Friend Wood did not follow up this

4

matter was that weightier affairs demanded his
immediate and entire attention.   One difficulty was overcome only to develop another.
No sooner had he silenced the cavils of the
farmers and demonstrated the value of his
patent, than infringements upon his rights
threatened to, and actually did, rob him of the
fruits of his invention.   "Uneasy rests the head
that wears a crown " of genius.

The patent laws of that day were very im-
perfect, and there was a strong prejudice
against their enforcement.   The cry of " no
monopoly " was raised.   Mr. Wood had ex-
pended many thousands of dollars in perfect-
ing his patterns and getting ready to supply
the demand which he felt sure would arise for
his plows, many of which, during the first
few years, he gave away, that their value might
be established to the satisfaction of the public.
The stage of probation over, the plow makers
of the country, defiant of patent law, engaged

in their manufacture. His patent had fourteen years to run. In an incredibly short
time their use by the farmers in all parts of
the land became almost universal, and had he
been allowed a royalty, however small, he
would have realized a vast fortune. Instead
of that he very nearly exhausted all his property in unavailing endeavors to establish
through the courts his rights as inventor and
patentee.

In 1833, when his patent expired, Congress
granted a renewal for fourteen years. He was
now bowed with the burden of years, and
debts incurred in trying to protect himself
against infringers. His remaining days were
spent in vain efforts to maintain his rights.
His broad and kindly nature had conceived
noble plans for the use of the wealth which at
one time seemed so nearly within his reach.
He had always been deeply interested in education, and had fortune smiled upon him it is

not too much to say that in spirit, however different in detail, Jethro Wood would have anticipated Stephen Girard, Ezra Cornell and John S. Hopkins, in nobly founding a great institution of learning.

In private life Jethro Wood was a model man. If he had faults it is impossible to ascertain them, for it would seem, from the concurrent testimony of all who were acquainted with him, that

> " None knew him but to love him,
> None name him but to praise."

Although a consistent member of the Society of Friends, Mr. Wood was extremely liberal in his religious views, and did not conform to the peculiar dress of the sect. He had that truly Catholic spirit so admirably characteristic of the great Quaker-poet, John G. Whittier. Not even the cruel wrongs he sustained at the hands of dishonest infringers could turn the sweetness of his kindly temper. Nature had endowed him richly in every way, and no gift had been abused. Physically, his was the highest type of manly beauty. Six feet and two inches in height, perfect in proportion, courtly in manner, his presence was worthy his character.

We will not linger over the closing scene of his eventful life. That belongs to the sacred secrecy of private grief. His death occurred at the very threshold of a new conflict, and upon it his son and executor, Benjamin Wood, entered with intelligent zeal. The closing of it being reserved for two of his daughters.

The story of these new labors was well told several years ago by a journalist familiar with the facts, and we cannot do better than to unearth the record from its musty file, and by transcribing it to these pages, give it a kind of resurrection worthy its importance.

"After the death of Jethro Wood, his son

Benjamin, who received the invention as a
legacy, continued his efforts to wrest justice
from the unwilling hand of the law. Nearly
all his father's failures had proceeded from the
inadequacy of the patent laws, which were
almost worthless to protect the rights of the
inventor. Even now a patent is worth little
until it it has been fought through the Supreme
Court of the United States. In those days so
many obstacles were thrown in the way of inventors, and the combinations against them
were so formidable, that Eli Whitney, in trying to establish his right to the cotton-gin in
a Georgia court, while his machine was doub-
ling and trebling the value of lands through
the State, had this experience, which is given
in his own words : I had great difficulty in
proving that the machine had been used in
Georgia, *although at the same moment there
were three separate sets of this machinery in
motion within fifty yards of the building in*

which the court sat, and all so near that the rattling of the wheels was distinctly heard on the steps of the Court House.

" Similar difficulties had met Jethro Wood in *his* suits; so his son resolved to strike at the root of the evil by securing a reform in the laws. He accordingly went to Washington, where he remained through several sessions, always working to this end. Clay, Webster, and John Quincy Adams, all of whom had known Jethro Wood and his invention, aided his son powerfully with their votes and counsel, and he succeeded in securing several important changes in the patent laws.

" Then he returned to New York, and commenced suit to resist encroachments on his right, and the wholesale manufacture of his plow by those who refused to pay the premium to the inventor. The " Cast-Iron Plow " was now used all over the country, and formidable combinations of its manufacturers united their

capital and influence against Benjamin Wood.
William H. Seward, then practicing law, was
retained as Wood's counsel, and the plow-
makers engaged all the talent they could mus-
ter to oppose him.

" Heretofore it had never been contradicted
that Jethro Wood was the originator of the
plow in use, but now his right to the invention
was denied, and it was alleged that his improvements had been forestalled by other
makers. Again and again the case was ad-
journed, and Europe and America were ran-
sacked for specimens of the different plows
which were declared to include his patent.

"Mr. Wood also obtained from England
samples of the plows of James Small and
Robert Ransom. He searched New-Jersey to
find the Peacock plow which was said to have
a cast-iron mould-board of exactly similar
shape to his father's. Everywhere in that
State he found ' Wood's plow ' in use, but he

could hear nothing of the one he sought. At length riding near a farm-house he discovered one of the old 'Newbold-Peacock plows' lying under a fence, dilapidated and rust-eaten. 'We don't use it any more,' the farmer replied to his inquiries, 'we've got one a good deal better.' 'Will you sell this?' asked Wood. 'Well, yes.' And Wood, glad to get it at almost any price, paid the keen farmer, who took advantage of his evident anxiety, two or three times the price of a new plow, and added the old one to his specimens.

"This motley collection of implements was brought into court and exhibited to the judges. At last, after the case had dragged its slow length along, through many terms, and the plaintiff was nearly worn out with the law's delay, the time for final trial and decision arrived. The combination of plow-makers feared that the case would go in Wood's favor, and made every effort to keep him out of court, that he might lose it by default. During his long entanglement in the law, he had contracted many debts, and one of his opponents had managed to purchase several of these accounts. Just before the case was to be heard for the last time, this worthy plow manufacturer, attended by a sheriff, and armed with a warrant to arrest Wood for debt, appeared at the front door of his house. Fortunately Wood had had a few minutes warning, and slipping out at the back door, he made his way under cover of approaching darkness to a house of a friendly neighbor. There he procured a horse and started for Albany, 150 miles distant, hearing every moment in fancy the clattering of hoofs at his heels.

"As if fortune could not be sufficiently ill-natured, his horse proved vicious and unmanageable, and thrice in the tedious journey threw the rider from his saddle upon the frozen earth, so injuring him, that he was barely able to go on.

" On arriving at Albany he found himself not a moment too soon. The case had an immediate hearing, and after three days' trial the Circuit Court decided unequivocally that the plow now in general use over the country was unlike any other which had been produced ; that the improvements which rendered it so effective were due to Jethro Wood, and that all manufacturers must pay his heirs for the privilege of making it.

"This was a great triumph; but it was now the late autumn of 1845, and the last grant of the patent had little more than a year to run. Wood again repaired to Washington to apply for a new extension, but the excitements of so long a contest had been too much for him. Just as he had recommenced his efforts they were forever ended. While talking with one of his friends, he suddenly fell dead from heart disease, and the patent expired without renewal.

" The last male heir to the invention was no
more. On settling the estate, it was found
that while not a vestige remained of the large
fortune owned by Jethro Wood when he began his career, *less than five hundred and
fifty dollars had ever been received from his
invention.*

" The after history of the case is a brief one.
Four daughters of Jethro Wood alone remained to represent the family. In the win-
ter of 1848 the two younger sisters went to
Washington to petition Congress that a bill
might be passed for their relief, in view of the
inestimable services of their father to the agricultural interests of the country. Webster declared that he regarded their father as a
'public benefactor,' and gave them his most
efficient aid ; Clay warmly espoused their
cause, and the venerable John Quincy Adams,
with his trembling hand—then so enfeebled
by age that he rarely used the pen—wrote
them kind notes, heartily sympathizing with

them. On one memorable day, while they were in the House gallery, Mr. Adams, at his desk on the floor, wrote them briefly in relation to their case. A few minutes later he was struck with the fatal attack under which he exclaimed, 'This is the last of earth; I am content,' and was borne dying to the Speaker's room. The tremulous lines, the last his hand ever traced, were found on his desk and delivered to Miss Wood.

"A bill providing that in these four heirs should rest for seven years the exclusive right of making and vending the improvements in the construction of the cast-iron plow ; and that twenty-five cents on each plow might be exacted from all who manufactured it, passed the Senate unanimously. But Washington already swarmed with plow manufacturers. The city of Pittsburgh alone sent five to look after their interests. Money was freely used, and the members of the House Com-

mittee who were to report on the bill were as-
sured that during the 28 years of the patent,
Wood's family had reaped immense wealth,
and wished to keep up a monopoly. The two
quiet ladies, fresh from the retirement of a
Quaker home, where they had learned little
of the world, were even accused of attempting
to secure its extention through bribery. It
was the wolf charging the lamb with roiling
the water. So ignorant were they of such
means, that, though the Chairman of the Com-
mittee plainly told the younger lady in a few
words of private conversation that a very few
thousand dollars would give her a favorable
verdict, she did not understand the suggestion
till after an unfavorable report was presented,
and the bill killed in the House.

" When they were about to leave Washington, some friendly members of Congress ad-
vised them to deposit the valuable documents
which had been used in their suit, including

the letter from Thomas Jefferson to Jethro Wood, in the archives of the House, where they could only be withdrawn on the motion of some member. They did so, and left them for some years uncalled for. When at last they applied for them they could not be found. Nor from that time to the present has any trace of them been discovered by any of the family. Thus perished the last vestige of proof relating to this ill-fated invention."

This is a fair and candid statement, one fully sustained by unimpeachable documentary evidence. Especially by the somewhat voluminous pamphlet entitled "Documents relating to the improvements of Jethro Wood in the Construction of the Plough." A careful examination of the testimony therein embodied, and of the Congressional Reports on the subject, warrant the foregoing statements.

It is not strange that in an early annual report of the United States Commissioner of

Agriculture, that official should have remarked
with some bitterness that "Although Wood
was one of the greatest benefactors to mankind
by this admirable invention, he never received,
for all his thought, anxiety and expense, a
sum of money sufficient to defray the expenses
of his decent burial." The time long since
passed forever to seek pecuniary indemnity;
but a debt of gratitude never outlaws, and it
is due to the great inventor that his country-
men should gratefully cherish his memory.
Every year adds to the debt we all owe him.
As the area of cultivation widens, the obliga-
tion deepens. Already America is the foremost nation of all the earth in the production
of wheat and provisions, the latter being in
reality corn in meat form. In exchange for
our food supplies, the United States is draining
Europe of its gold at an enormous rate, and
the fundamental element in the production of
American wealth, is our great implement of

tillage. American prosperity is the monumental glory of Jethro Wood and his plow.

"The Balance Sheet of the World" shows that the United States can boast more acres of tillage, in proportion to population, than any other country on the globe; and in grain production, outstrips all competitors. Of such a record every American citizen may well be proud, and it should be remembered that without the genius of Wood such a record could not have been made, even approximately. But in order to a just appreciation of the importance of the modern plow and the usefulness of the inventor of it, one should take a retrospective glance, tracing, as best we may without tedious details, the steps which led from the use of a forked stick to the present implement for fallowing the ground. The *Scientific American*, which ought to be good authority on such a subject, in speaking of the Wood patent, says: "Previously the plow was a

5

stick of wood plated with iron." If this does
sound like an exaggeration, but is really a
plain statement of fact, consider for a moment
what the plow really is in its relation to civil-
. ization.

The savage lives by the chase and upon the bounty of untilled nature. The first
steps toward civilization are to domesticate an-
imals, and cultivate the soil with a rude kind
of hoe. Both are alike primitive. The next
step is to press the beast into service by sup-
plementing the hoe with a plow. In that
implement we see what might be called the
original strand in the mighty cord which binds
in co-operation man, brute and earth. By
means of this agency of agriculture the beast
of the field is made to toil, and purchases the
benefits of human kindness at the expense of
idleness and industry. It is not too much, then,
to say that the plow is at once " the tie that
binds," and the tap-root which nourishes the

the world. If by some miraculous calamity this one implement were forever swept away, universal and unappeasable famine would be inevitable. And that occasional famines of a local character are disappearing from the civilized world, is very largely, if not chiefly, due to the improved tillage resulting from improved plows.

We might well say, in paraphrase of a familiar saying attributed to Napoleon: Let me make the plows of a nation, and I care not who makes their laws.

The primitive plow was and is (for the barbarian of to-day is substantially the same in his agricultural methods as the barbarian of antiquity) simply a forked stick, to which is attached by a strip of rawhide or a wisp of grass, a beast, often the patient cow. As the prong passes over the ground, held down by the bowed form of the poor tiller, it barely scratches the face of the earth.

The first improvement was to reverse the stick and notch the forward end. By that means the animal could be more securely fas-' tened to the plow, the thong being tied around the crotch of the stick. The shorter limb ran along the surface of the ground, the notch in front being the only reliance for stirring the soil. In the absence of a compact turf, such plowing would do a little good in rendering the ground fallow, and would at least have the merit of not being so difficult to operate as its predecessor.

The third plow had three parts. It consisted of a beam, a handle and a share, all constructed by simply trimming the natural wood selected for that purpose. In the first plow the prong which served as a share was slanting, while in the third it rested flatly upon the ground, projecting forward, instead of backward, as in the second plow. It could have required no very difficult search to have found small trees and broken limbs, needing no mechanical skill in fashioning, to render them serviceable for such crude uses. They may be termed nature's contribution to the art of plow-making.

Without going further into details, it may be stated that a standard authority on the history of mechanism asserts that "the ancient Egyptian, Etruscan, Syrian, and Greek plows, were equal to the modern plows of the south of France, part of Austria, Poland, Sweden, Spain, Turkey, Persia, Arabia, India, Ceylon and China); at least such was the case until the middle of the present century." The Roman and Gallic plows were better than those of the modern countries named. The Gauls had mould-board plows. Pliny is our authority for this statement. That eminent Latin author of eighteen centuries ago, in speaking on the general subject, says:

"Plows are of various kinds. The colter is

the iron part which cuts the thick sod before
it is broken into pieces and traces beforehand
by its incision the future furrows, which the
share, reversed, is to open with its teeth.
Another kind, the common plowshare, is
nothing more than a lever furnished with a
pointed beak ; while another variety, which is
used in light, easy soils, does not present an
edge projecting from the share-beam through-
out, but only a small point at the extremity.
In a fourth kind, again, this point is larger
and formed with a cutting edge by the agency
of which it cleaves the ground, and by the
sharp edges at the side cuts up the weeds by
the roots."

Pliny adds that the broader the plowshare
the better it is for turning up the soil.   These
excerpts from the great Roman may serve to
show the utmost reach of invention in that
line, until a new impulse, begun in the Nether-
lands in the eighteenth century, was brought

to perfect development in the next century by an American citizen who died the poorer for his invention.

The highest of all authorities upon this and cognate subjects is "Knight's American Mechanical Dictionary," and Knight says of Jethro Wood, "He made the best plows up to date." He adds, "He met with great opposition, and then with much injustice, losing a competency in introducing his plow and fighting infringers." The same writer defines the peculiarities of the Wood plow with remarkable clearness and brevity: "It consisted in the mode of securing the cast-iron portions together by lugs and locking pieces, doing away with screw-bolts, and much weight, complexity and expense. It was the first plow in which the parts most exposed to wear could be renewed in the field by the substitution of cast pieces." Considering the source of this passage, it may be said that literature

could hardly pay a nobler tribute to the
memory of Jethro Wood than this. It is
doubly significant, from the fact that Knight's
publishers, Houghton, Osgood & Co., are also
the publishers of the *Atlantic Monthly*, in
the May number of which magazine a *habitue*
of the National Capital tried to belittle the
invention of Jethro Wood, and malign as iniquitous the attempt of his daughters, cham-
pioned by John Quincy Adams, to secure for
that invention proper recognition. It would
be quite superfluous to follow this maligner in
the details of this, and a subsequent attack in
an agricultural journal. He disclaims any
design to defame the claimants, but insists
that other and earlier inventors deserve the
credit for the modern plow. The opinion of
Knight's Dictionary upon the Wood patent
has just been given, and the following extract
from the same great work sets forth in their
proper relations to the modern plow the in-

ventions of those for whom this *habitue* makes preposterous claims :

" The modern plow," says Knight, " originated in the low countries, so-called. Flanders and Holland gave to England much of her husbandry and gardening knowledge, field, kitchen and ornamental. Blythe's 'Improver Improved,' published in 1652, has allusions to the subject. Lummis, in 1720, imported plows from Holland. James Small, of Berwickshire, Scotland, made plows and wrote treatises on the subject, 1784. He made cast-iron mold-boards and wrought-iron shares, and introduced the draft-chain. He made shares of cast-iron in 1785. The importation of what was known as the 'Rotherham' plow was the immediate cause of the improvement in plows which dates from the middle of the last century. Whether the name is derived from Rotterdam cannot be determined.

" The American plow, during the colonial period, was of wood, the mold-board being covered with sheet-iron, or plates made by hammering out old horseshoes. Jefferson studied and wrote on the subject, to determine the proper shape of the mold-board. He treated it as consisting of a lifting and an up-setting wedge, with an easy connecting curve. Newbold, of New Jersey, in 1797, patented a plow with a mold-board, share and land side all cast together. Peaccok, in his patent of 1807, cast his plow in three pieces, the point of the colter entering a notch in the breast of the share."

It will be observed that the credit given these improvers of the plow is very considerable, without at all trenching upon the exceptional credit due to Jethro Wood. With such an authoritative refutation, the slander may well be dismissed as beneath further notice.

In no way more appropriately can final leave be taken of the subject in hand than by presenting the apostrophe to Jethro Wood from the pen of Edward Webster, formerly associated editor of the *Rural New Yorker:*

No jeweled diadem or crown
  E'er glittered on thy manly brow—
No slave would tremble at thy frown,
  Nor at thy footstool bow;
For thou wert pure in heart and mind,
And strove to *raise*—not crush mankind!

As famed Prometheus of yore,
  In aid of our lost, wretched sires,
Stole from the flaming sun, and bore
  Down to the earth those fires
That fill with light and life all space,
And mark the Day God's glorious race—

So thy inventive genius found
  For man the bright and polished share,
That bids the willing fields abound
  With fruits beyond compare;
And from the seed that falls like rain
Crowds full our barns with bearded grain!

Eternal may the honors shine,
   We yield with grateful hearts to thee;
May children's children round thy shrine—
   Sons of the brave and free—
With reverent lips pronounce thy name,
   And build for thee a deathless fame!

www.ingramcontent.com/pod-product-compliance
Lightning Source LLC
Chambersburg PA
CBHW030017030726
47499CB00008B/3031